# Adeline Porcupine

## BY CHARLES GHIGNA
### ILLUSTRATED BY JACQUELINE EAST

PICTURE WINDOW BOOKS
a capstone imprint

*For Charlotte Rose*

Tiny Tales are published by Picture Window Books,
a Capstone imprint
1710 Roe Crest Drive
North Mankato, Minnesota 56003
www.capstonepub.com

Library of Congress Cataloging-in-Publication Data
Ghigna, Charles, author.
Adeline Porcupine  / by Charles Ghigna ; illustrated by Jacqueline
East.pages cm. — (Tiny tales)

Summary: Sweet-natured Adeline Porcupine is feeling a little left
out because all the other animals are cautious because of her sharp
quills--but with a little help from Danny Armadillo she joins in the
play and makes friends.

ISBN 978-1-4795-6530-6 (library binding)
ISBN 978-1-4795-6534-4 (paperback)
ISBN 978-1-4795-8481-9 (eBook)

1.  Porcupines--Juvenile fiction. 2.  Animals--Juvenile fiction.
3.  Friendship--Juvenile fiction. 4.  Play--Juvenile fiction. [1.
Porcupines--Fiction. 2. Animals--Fiction. 3. Friendship--Fiction.
4. Play--Fiction.]  I. East, Jacqueline, illustrator. II. Title.
PZ7.G3390234Ad 2016

 [E]--dc23                                        2014045633

Designer: Kristi Carlson

# table of contents

# A Best Friend

Adeline Porcupine was sad.

"I have a lot of friends," she said. "I just wish I had a best friend."

Adeline knew all her friends liked her. But she also knew they would not get close to her because of her sharp quills.

"I wish I had a friend who wasn't afraid of my quills," she said.

Adeline Porcupine waddled outside. She sat on the front step. It was autumn. Leaves were clinging to the trees, riding the breeze, and falling to the ground.

Adeline watched as her friends played.

Sally Squirrel and Sarah Skunk were holding hands and singing. Burt Beaver and Peter Possum were playing leapfrog. Molly Mouse and Chipper Chipmunk were racing around a tree.

"Everyone has a best friend but me," said Adeline Porcupine.

"Let's all play hide-and-seek," yelled Danny Armadillo.

"Can I play, too?" she asked.

"Of course!" said Danny.

Adeline Porcupine was excited. She quickly waddled over to play.

"I will count to ten, so hide fast," he said.

Everyone ran in different directions. Each animal was looking for a special place to hide.

"One. Two. Three . . ."

Adeline Porcupine hid under the rose bush. She loved rose bushes. They had sharp thorns, which were like her sharp quills.

*No one will find me here*, she thought, smiling.

Just then, she felt something tap her
shoulder.

"Found you!" said Danny.

Adeline Porcupine couldn't believe it.
No friend had ever gotten so close to her.

As Adeline Porcupine got up from her hiding place, she lost her balance. She fell right on top of Danny. His thick shell protected him from her quills.

The other friends had come out of their hiding places.

"New game! Let's jump in leaf piles," said Burt Beaver.

The friends worked hard to make a big leaf pile. They raked and raked. Every leaf was swept into the big pile.

"Who wants to jump first?" asked Burt.

"Me!" said Adeline. She was so happy she couldn't hold back. She ran and jumped into a huge pile of leaves.

"Who's next?" asked Burt.

"Not me," said Chipper Chipmunk.

"Not me," said Molly Mouse.

"Not me!" said Sally Squirrel and Sarah Skunk.

Nobody wanted to jump with Adeline because of her quills. But Adeline didn't have time to get sad.

"Look out!" said Danny Armadillo. He ran and jumped into the leaves right next to Adeline.

The pile exploded with color as Danny and Adeline jumped and danced and rolled and laughed.

"What do you know?" Adeline said. "I finally found a best friend."

"Yes, you did," said Danny. "And so did I."

## 2

# Special Tricks

Adeline Porcupine took a deep breath, puffed out her quills, and took off. She ran backward right into the side of an empty cardboard box. Her sharp quills poked holes in the box like a dozen darts.

"Wow!" said Danny Armadillo. "I wish I could do that!"

Danny had heard that porcupines could run backward when they wanted to use their quills. This was the first time he had seen a porcupine do it. It was amazing!

"What tricks can you do?" Adeline asked.

"I can roll myself up into a ball," said Danny.

"How do you do that?" asked Adeline.

"It's easy. Watch!" Danny said. Then he curled up into a ball and rolled himself inside the box.

"That is a cool trick," said Adeline.

Molly Mouse strolled by. "What are you guys doing?"

"We're showing each other cool tricks we can do," said Adeline Porcupine.

"Do you have any special tricks you can do?" Danny asked.

"I can make elephants disappear," said Molly Mouse.

"No way," said Danny.

"Yes, I can," she said. "You don't see any elephants around here, do you?"

Adeline and Danny laughed at Molly's joke.

Burt Beaver and Peter Possum heard Adeline's laughter.

"What's going on?" asked Peter.

"We're showing each other cool tricks we can do," said Adeline Porcupine.

"What special things can you and Burt do?" Danny asked.

Peter Possum said, "Well, I can hang by my tail. Watch!"

Peter scampered up a tree. Then he showed how he could hang by his tail.

"That is cool," said Adeline.

"I can turn a stream into a pond," said Burt Beaver.

"How do you do that?" asked Adeline.

"I chew sticks with my big teeth. Then I use the sticks to build a dam," said Burt.

"That is a cool trick!" said Adeline.

"What's a cool trick?" asked Sarah Skunk.

"We're talking about tricks we can do," said Adeline.

"What cool tricks can you do?" asked Danny.

"I can do magic," Sarah Skunk said.

"Like the trick Molly Mouse can do with elephants?" asked Danny.

"No. Real magic. I just use my magic wand," said Sarah Skunk.

"Your magic wand?" asked Adeline.

"Yes, my big bushy tail is a magic wand. All I have to do is wave it, and everyone runs away," said Sarah.

Everyone burst out laughing.

"That is definitely the coolest trick of all," said Adeline.

# 3

# A New You

Adeline Porcupine and Sally
Squirrel strolled through the park.
Burt Beaver was down by the creek.
Peter Possum was in a big oak tree.
Chipper Chipmunk was in the
sandbox. Molly Mouse and Sarah
Skunk were on the swings. Danny
Armadillo was on the slide.

"Do you ever wonder what it would be like to be a different animal?" asked Adeline.

"What do you mean?" asked Sally.

"You know. If you could be any animal in the whole world, who would you want to be?" Adeline asked.

"Well, I never thought about it," said Sally. "But it sounds like fun!"

"What sounds like fun?" asked Peter. He was hanging upside down by his tail from the limb of a tree just above their heads.

"Adeline was wondering who she would like to be if she could be somebody else," said Sally.

"Like a new you," Adeline said.

"A new you? That does sound like fun! Can I play, too?" asked Peter.

"Sure," said Adeline.

"Maybe the others would like to play," said Sally.

"Hey, everyone!" shouted Peter. "We're about to play a new game."

"What game?" asked Danny as everyone came running over.

"It's called A New You. Adeline just made it up," said Sally.

"What do we do?" Chipper asked.

"You just say who you would like to be and why," said Adeline.

"That sounds like fun," said Chipper. "Can I go first?"

"Sure!" said Adeline.

"I wonder what it would be like to be an eagle," said Chipper. "It would be fun to fly."

"I wonder what it would be like to be a bear. I would love to sleep all winter," said Burt.

"I wonder what it would be like to be a dog," said Molly Mouse. "It would be fun to have someone pet and feed me every day."

"I wonder what it would be like to be a zebra. I could keep my black-and-white stripes," said Sarah Skunk.

"I wonder what it would be like to be a different color," Adeline said. "I wish I could be a beautiful peacock. I would have colorful feathers instead of black-and-white quills."

"I can fix that," said Danny. He waddled over to the bushes and picked flowers. Then he put them on Adeline's quills.

"Wow!" said everyone.

"You look beautiful with all those flowers," said Sally. "But you look beautiful without them, too."

"Thank you," said Adeline. "What would you like to be, Sally?"

"It's fun wondering about who we want to be. But I think you all will agree, I just want to be me!" Sally Squirrel said.

Everyone nodded and laughed. Sally's perfect rhyme was the perfect end to their day of wonders.

# Bursting with Joy

Adeline Porcupine was excited. It was a beautiful day, and she was going to play at the park.

As she got closer to the park, she saw her friends standing in a line.

"Hooray! It's Adeline Porcupine," they yelled. "Come over and see this!"

At the front of the line stood a kangaroo with lots and lots of colorful balloons.

He was making balloon animals! He gave a red dog to Burt Beaver.

"Woof! Woof!" said Burt.

The kangaroo made another balloon animal. It was a blue horse.

"Neigh!" said Peter Possum.

Then he made a pink bunny for Sarah Skunk.

"I love it! Hop, hop, hop," said Sarah.

The kangaroo made a green dinosaur next. He gave it to Danny Armadillo.

"Roar!" said Danny.

Adeline Porcupine couldn't wait to see what balloon animal the kangaroo would make for her!

He worked extra hard on her balloon. He turned and twisted a long yellow balloon into a giraffe.

"This one's for you," he said.

"Look at my giraffe!" she said.

This was Adeline's first ever balloon animal. In fact, this was her first ever balloon!

She held her yellow giraffe balloon
over her head to show everyone. POP!

"Oh, no!" said Adeline Porcupine.
"My quills have popped my balloon."

"Don't be sad, Adeline. Balloons
never last very long, even if you don't
have quills to pop them," said Danny.

"Look, Adeline," said Peter Possum. "I have something even better than a balloon to play with."

Peter pulled out a folded up beach ball from his pocket. He began to blow it up. He blew and blew and blew until the multi-colored beach ball was as round as a pumpkin.

Then Peter tossed the ball in the air.
All of the friends joined in, hitting the
ball to keep it off the ground.

"I love this new game," said Danny.

"My turn!" said Burt Beaver. He
gave the beach ball a big whack with
his tail. The ball went soaring above
the crowd. Then it drifted back down,
heading straight for Adeline.

Adeline was afraid to take her turn. She didn't want to pop the ball. She just had to be gentle.

She waited and waited as the big beach ball floated down. Then, as softly as she could, she hit it into the air. But it wasn't soft enough. POP!

"Oh, dear! I've done it again!" cried Adeline. "I'm so sorry, Peter. I didn't mean to ruin your ball. My quills just keep getting in the way."

"It's okay, Adeline," said Peter Possum. "There are many other games we can play."

"Look what I have," said Sarah Skunk. She pulled a big jar of bubbles from her backpack. "Let's see who can pop the most!"

They raced out to the open field. Sarah Skunk blew lots of bubbles high up into the air.

"Ha! That's easy. I know who can pop the most bubbles," said Danny.

Burt, Peter, Sarah, and Danny watched Adeline race around the field. Her long, sharp quills popped big batches of bubbles before they hit the ground.

Adeline sat down under a tree. She was tired and sticky from popping so many bubbles.

"Adeline Porcupine is our all-time bubble-popping champion!" said Danny.

"Oh, my," said Adeline. "That was so much fun! Now it's time to go home and take a bath."

"Yes," laughed Danny. "A big bubble bath!"

# Glossary

autumn (AW-tuhm) — the season between summer and winter, from late September to late December. Also called fall.

balance (BAL-uhnss) — the ability to keep yourself steady and from falling over

batches (BACH-ehss) — groups of things that are made at the same time or arrive together

champion (CHAM-pee-uhn) — the winner of a contest

dam (DAM) — a wall that stops the flow of a river or stream

exploded (ek-SPLOD-ed) — burst out with great force

protected (pro-TEKT-ed) — guarded or made safe

quill (KWIL) — one of the many long, sharp, and pointed spines on a porcupine

ruin (ROO-in) — to destroy or wreck something

scampered (SKAM-purd) — ran quickly and lightly

strolled (STROHLD) — walked in a slow and relaxed way

trick (TRIK) — a skillful or clever act

wonders (WUHN-durs) — things that are so special or impressive that they cause you to be amazed

# Discussion Questions

1. Adeline knew she had friends, but she wanted to have a best friend. Would you rather have lots of friends or one best friend? Talk about your choice.

2. The animal friends showed off their special tricks. Do you have any special talents or tricks? Did you have to practice to learn how to do your trick?

3. Adeline Porcupine popped Peter Possum's beach ball, but he forgave her because it was an accident and she was sorry. Talk about a time you forgave someone. How did you feel? Was it hard or easy?

4. Adeline was the bubble-popping champion. What are you really good at?

5. The animal friends played lots of games like leapfrog, hide-and-seek, and tossing around a beach ball. Talk about your favorite game to play.

6. Adeline Porcupine tries to be careful because her quills can pop things very easily. Have you ever had to be gentle with something to make sure you didn't break or hurt it? Talk about it.

# Writing Prompts

1. There are lots fun things to do in autumn. Adeline and her friends raked up a pile of leaves and then jumped in it! Make a list of things you like to do during the fall.

2. Adeline pretended to be a peacock. If you could be any animal, which one would you be? Write a paragraph about why you picked your animal.

3. This book takes place during autumn. Which season is your favorite: autumn, winter, summer, or spring? Draw a picture of the season and then write why it's your favorite.

4. The animal friends had fun playing on the swings and slides in the park. Write your own story about you and your friends having a good time at the park.

5. Adeline made up a game called A New You. Think of a new game for you and your friends to play. Write down the rules and how to play.

6. The animal friends spend a lot of time outside. Write about your favorite thing to do when you're outside.

# Author Bio

Charles Ghigna (also known as Father Goose®) lives in a tree house in Alabama. He is the author of more than 100 award-winning books for children and adults from Random House, Capstone, Disney, Hyperion, Scholastic, Simon & Schuster, Abrams, Charlesbridge, and other publishers.

His poems appear in hundreds of magazines from *The New Yorker* and *Harper's* to *Cricket* and *Highlights*. He is a former poetry editor of the *English Journal* and nationally syndicated feature writer for Tribune Media Services.

# Illustrator Bio

Jacqueline East has been illustrating children's books for many years. Her work has been published across the globe and is known for its warm innocence and humor. Everything is an inspiration, and she especially loves the golden atmosphere of twilight; a magical time of day that is often the backdrop for her characters.

She has worked above a chocolate factory, in a caravan by the sea, and now, from her home in Bristol with Scampi the dog sleeping in the corner of the studio.